P9-ELS-886

Ladybug
Girl
and the
Big Snow

by David Soman and
Jacky Davis

Dial Books for Young Readers

an imprint of Penguin Group (USA) Inc.

For Amy, Hugh, and the magical Niall Alexander Sicotte

DIAL BOOKS FOR YOUNG READERS
A division of Penguin Young Readers Group
Published by the Penguin Group
Penguin Group (USA) Inc., 375 Hudson Street, New York, New York 10014, USA

USA | Canada | UK | Ireland | Australia | New Zealand | India | South Africa | China
Penguin Books Ltd, Registered Offices: 80 Strand, London WC2R 0RL, England

For more information about the Penguin Group visit penguin.com

Text copyright © 2013 by Jacky Davis
Pictures copyright © 2013 by David Soman

All rights reserved. No part of this book may be reproduced, scanned, or distributed in any printed or electronic
form without permission. Please do not participate in or encourage piracy of copyrighted materials
in violation of the author's rights. Purchase only authorized editions.

Library of Congress Cataloging-in-Publication Data
Soman, David.
Ladybug Girl and the big snow / by David Soman and Jacky Davis.
pages   cm
Summary: Wearing her ladybug costume, Lulu plays in new fallen snow.
ISBN 978-0-8037-3583-5 (hardcover)
[1. Snow—Fiction. 2. Imagination—Fiction.] I. Davis, Jacky, date. II. Title.
PZ7.S696224Lbp 2013
[E]—dc23   2012033451

Manufactured in China on acid-free paper
1 3 5 7 9 10 8 6 4 2

Designed by Jasmin Rubero
Text set in Old Claude LP Regular

The publisher does not have any control over and does not assume
any responsibility for author or third-party websites or their content.

ALWAYS LEARNING   PEARSON

"It's magic outside, Bingo," whispers Lulu.
"Everything is covered in snow!"

Lulu can't wait to explore,

but first she puts on her long johns,

snow pants,

boots,

puffy jacket,

and mittens.

After she puts on her earmuffs, tutu, and wings, she is finally ready.

It's a little hard to move,

but that won't stop Ladybug Girl.

The silvery sun bounces off the snow and makes the yard
look like it's filled with giant frosted cakes.

Ladybug Girl tries some of the frosting.
It's pretty good. Bingo thinks so too.

Ladybug Girl and Bingo walk across her yard.

It's fun to go where no one else has.

They walk all over.

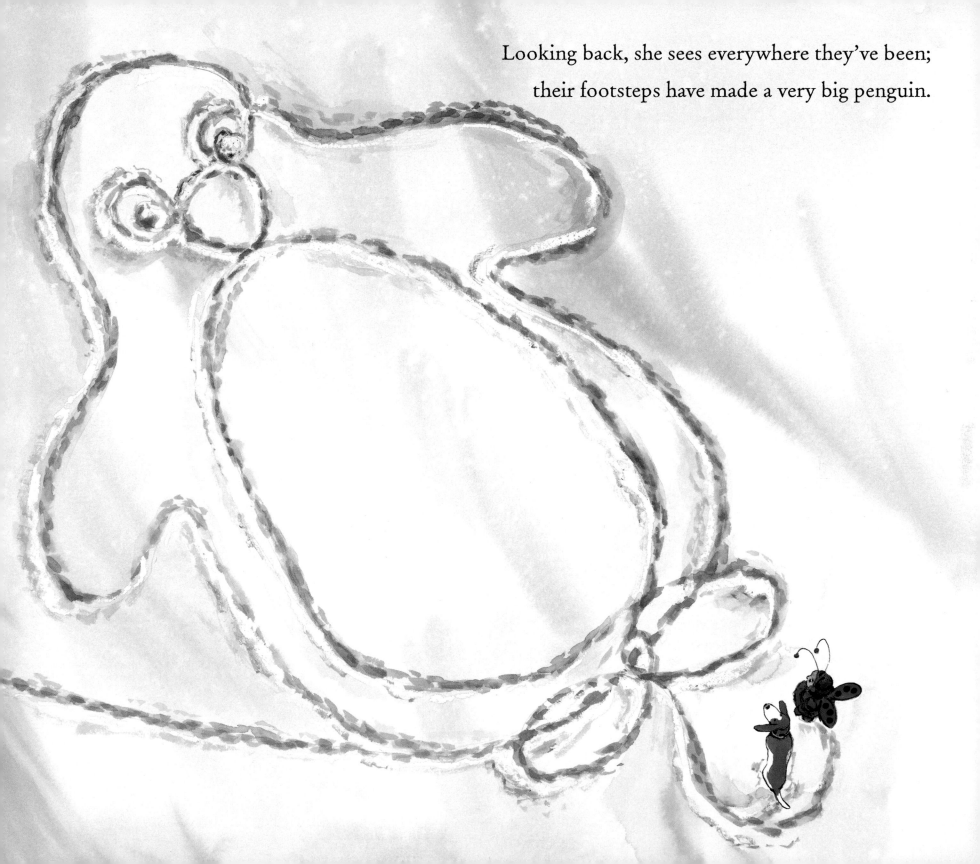

Looking back, she sees everywhere they've been;
their footsteps have made a very big penguin.

When she moves, Lulu can hear her pants and jacket whistling. When she stands still, she can hear the trees creaking in the wind. A few dry leaves that cling to the branches ring like little bells. It sounds like music.

Out in the middle of the yard, Lulu notices the sun glinting off the snowman her brother is making.

And *then* the entire castle wall collapses into a big pile of snow.

"Oh, I give up!"

Lulu abandons the snow castle and marches off toward the big pine trees at the back of the yard.

As she gets closer, she realizes
the trees look like **Snow Giants**.

She must stop them before they eat all the **snow cakes!**

Lulu knows her brother would **love** this game.
She tries to get his attention and accidentally whacks a branch,
knocking a shelf of snow onto her head
and down the back of her neck.
Her antennas get very bent out of shape.
Lulu wishes she could make *all* the snow disappear.

She huffs off toward home and sees her own white breath fuming like dragon smoke.

She is a dragon! And so is Bingo!

They are winter dragons soaring high above the glittering land.

Her fire is so hot, she could melt all the snow.

Then Lulu sees a high, snowy mountain peak;
it's the perfect place for the dragons to have their home.

They are flying toward the top when suddenly
Lulu sinks into the snow up to her tutu.

Why does everything have to be so hard today?
All she wanted to do was go to the top of the mountain,
and now she's stuck in the snow.
She's not even a flying dragon anymore;
she's just herself.

Lulu looks down at her stuck legs and notices the shadow
of her wings gliding over the surface of the snow.

She's **not** just Lulu, she's Ladybug Girl,
and Ladybug Girl can do anything!
Nothing is going to keep her from
getting where she wants to go.

Using all her might, she lifts her leg
out of the heavy snow and steps forward.
Then she lifts her other leg, and slowly and steadily
she begins to climb up, and up, and up farther still.

And then with a final lunge,
Ladybug Girl emerges on the top.
"We did it, Bingo!" Ladybug Girl yells.
"We made it!"

When she looks down she sees, shining in the sun,
right where her snow castle was supposed to be,
an amazing statue of . . .

Bingo!

"Look, Bingo," Ladybug Girl cries,
"we made a snow statue of you, and we didn't even know it!"

Ladybug Girl flies down the hill,

rushing toward the snow Bingo, and lands at the bottom

in a cloud of snow. The mountain seems so small now.

It's funny how one thing can change into another, just like that.

Ladybug Girl looks at her creation; it really is very excellent.
She should probably have Mama come out and take pictures of it for the newspaper.

Her brother comes over to see what she's doing,
and Ladybug Girl shows him the snow Bingo.
"That *is* pretty good," he says.
"I have an idea," says Ladybug Girl.
"Let's make lots of snow animals!"

They make enough for a whole forest.

When the sun starts to dip behind the trees, Ladybug Girl,
her brother, and Bingo head toward home.
Their shadows slip in and out of all the other shadows.
"Look," she says to her brother, "everything is connected."

Later, after Lulu changes out of her wet clothes,

she drinks hot chocolate with her brother by the fire.

As the sky turns a deeper blue, and the snow sifts down,
Ladybug Girl looks out the window and says,
"Snow really is magic, isn't it?"